D1404301

Dedicated to my loving family,
Keith, Tanner, and Samantha.

And to my inspiration,
Sequoia.

Dream BIG & Inspire Others!

Rikki Lynn Smith
2018

In the Woods

www.mascotbooks.com

Summer the Firefly

©2018 Vikki Lynn Smith. All Rights Reserved. No part of this publication may be reproduced, stored in a retrieval system or transmitted in any form by any means electronic, mechanical, or photocopying, recording or otherwise without the permission of the author.

For more information, please contact:
Mascot Books
620 Herndon Parkway, Suite 320
Herndon, VA 20170
info@mascotbooks.com

Library of Congress Control Number: 2018901596

CPSIA Code: PRT0418A
ISBN-13: 978-1-68401-524-5

Printed in the United States

SUMMER
THE FIREFLY

Written by
Vikki Lynn Smith

Illustrated by
Marcela Werkema

It was a hot, humid evening. The sun set far in the distance as the moon popped its head above the trees. High in the sky, branches lazily swayed in the gentle breeze that picked up and faded peacefully away.

Birds **snuggled** deep within their nests after a tiring day of flying lessons in the hot midday sun. Across the meadow, gurgling sounds played musically from the rock creek over the hill. **In the Woods**, everyone was at peace with the world.

King Deer moved quietly through the dense brush as he checked on the animals of the Woods. Their community had grown since he had first arrived to the clearing as a knob-kneed fawn. Now he stood well above the bramble bush and fallen branches. His large antlers brushed low canopies of young White Oak trees while he walked. He was big now, and the animals looked to him to protect them from dangers, whatever they might be.

King Dear had come to love the Woods over the years, and could not imagine a more perfect place to live. All about him were his friends—the rabbits, squirrels, birds, foxes, and even his dear friend Sequoia, the golden retriever from the house near the Woods. The trees and flowers had become a part of his family, too.

He loved them all dearly.

This evening, King Deer had a feeling something special was about to happen as he tread silently through the Woods. He wasn't certain what it would be, but there was something in the air that made his hair stand on end. He hoped whatever lay ahead would be worthy of a story he could tell his children.

Off in the distance, there was a sudden glow from out of the darkness that hushed the sounds of nature. But it disappeared as fast as it had come, and darkness swallowed its place once more. Without warning, a nearby tree frog sounded a call for all his neighbors to hear.

"G-G-Great news! G-G-Great news!"

His voice echoed through the Woods.
"The firefly has been born!"

The Woods were ablaze with noise as a chorus of shouts and cheers of joy came from the insects and animals.

"Yay! Hip, hip, hooray!"

The crickets and cicadas played their merry violins in excitement as their music filled the Woods for all to hear.

Waiting along with the others for the small glow bug to reappear, King Deer made his way to the center of attention.

Sequoia, who had heard the music of the Woods from her home, rushed out to join King Deer in the excitement. She loved being a part of this small community and stood with her tail wagging in anticipation.

"Quiet please," chirped Mother Blue Jay, flapping her wings for silence. "We must make certain that our dear Mr. Frog has indeed seen the glowing bug and not the flicker of man's fire."

Mr. Frog puffed his cheeks and let out a slow **Grib-bit!** "I daresay, Mother Blue Jay, I should think I would know the difference between a glow bug and human fire! Open your eyes, my dear friends, and let us search the darkness for the glow!"

Once again, the Woods **buzzed** with the sound of creatures eagerly awaiting news.

On a red-tipped bush, not far from Mr. Groundhog's hole, a spark flashed briefly before vanishing into the night. Cardinal Red saw it from above and chirped with excitement, "Firefly, firefly born on this day...everyone who's seen it say **hip, hip, hooray!**"

Why, everyone sang out in unison,
"Hip, hip, hooray!"
and the Woods came alive as if it were day.

Then, in the midst of the festivities, a small voice was heard. "Why is everyone so excited?"

The
firefly sat
ever so gently on
her red-tipped velvet leaf.
She looked about, surveying
the celebration occurring around
her. Her eyes spied raccoons chasing
each other across a fallen tree, a deer
prancing about smelling the air, and, high above
in the tall oak tree, an owl puffing his chest, readying
himself to speak.

"Dear friends of the Woods, please settle yourselves.
Our newest friend has spoken and still we converse so
loudly that we have missed her query!"

Little Squirrelin was confused. "What did Mr. Owl say, Mama?"

"He said the glow bug has spoken and we were too loud to hear,"
she whispered.

"Oh," replied Little Squirrelin.

"Dear little glow bug," Mr. Owl began,
"on behalf of myself and my fellow friends, I wish
you a warm welcome!"

"Welcome!" came cries echoing through every nook and
cranny of the Woods. The glow bug flapped her wings
and showered the Woods with her light.

"Thank you, everyone. You are all so kind. How
wonderful that you should greet all new creatures
of the Woods with such joy!"

Mr. Fox swished his red tail this way and that as he pranced beneath the glow bug.

"It is only for the birth of the first firefly that the creatures of the Woods celebrate," Mr. Fox began. "For this is the day that is most special to those who have survived the long winter and the many rains of spring. You, my little friend, our little glow bug, are the first firefly to grace the night skies of summer...and it is you who we give the name Summer."

The little firefly fluttered above her red velvet carpet and pondered the news she had just been given.

King Deer watched as the animals moved in to look at the small creature who had brought such delight to the Woods.

"I like the name Summer...but why am I so special?" she asked.

Perched on a nearby Loblolly pine, a woodpecker nibbled on an insect hidden deep within the bark of the tree. He turned and spoke to the little glowing bug.

"Why, the legend says that if a creature of the Woods is alive to witness the birth of the first firefly of the year, winter is officially over and the rainy spring season has passed. Life should be celebrated by all because the summer brings an easier way of life for everyone. There is more food and more sun..."

"...and more fun!" chimed in Sequoia.

The audience of animals and insects merrily broke out in laughter. Summer joined in, laughing her first laugh.

The Squirrelin family gathered around and joined in
the celebration, as did the birds who had heard the commotion
high in the trees. The animals began to sing a chorus in delight.

"Summer is here, Summer is here...
she's glowing in the Woods for all who are near.
Let us rejoice, be happy and cheer.
She's the first firefly we have seen this year."

Summer smiled at all her new friends, then flapped her wings, revealing the
prettiest yellow glow they had ever seen. She was happy to know that she had
found a home within the Woods where she would have friends and be loved.

And so it was, that the crickets, cicadas, and tree frogs did play a tune all night long until the next day. Summer the firefly was special indeed, for her glow shined for life in the darkness of the trees.

DID YOU KNOW...

Scientific Name: Lampyrida

Nickname: Firefly, Lightning Bug

Diet: Omnivore

Life Span: Up to 2 months

Size: Up to 1 inch

Location: Around the world, in wooded areas with higher rates of moisture

Best known for: *Bioluminescence* – light emitting from abdomen in a series of sequences based on species and gender

The firefly lays eggs in soil and under bark where they turn into larvae. The larvae are known as glowworms. The glowworm eats snails, slugs, and worms until it reaches adulthood. The adult firefly has such a short life that it is uncertain what they eat. It is believed they eat pollen, bugs, and nectar.

The adult firefly's light comes from under their abdomen. It is not a "hot light" but rather a "cold light" that is produced by a light organ. The light organ must have oxygen to glow and nitric acid to flash. The flash is significant as it serves at least two purposes: to attract a mate and to warn predators that their body is toxic and fatal if eaten. Each species of firefly has its own sequence of flashes. The chemicals in the firefly have been used successfully in medical research, and a synthetic (man-made) copy of the chemicals has been created.

Interesting Fact: The firefly's eggs glow!

For more information, activities, and lesson plans,
go to VikkiLynnSmith.com

REFERENCES

http://www.nationalgeographic.com/animals/invertebrates/group/fireflies/
http://www.firefly.org/
https://www.scientificamerican.com/article/how-and-why-do-fireflies/

ABOUT THE AUTHOR

Vikki Lynn Smith's love for writing began when she was very young as she chronicled living and traveling around the world. She has climbed the Washington Monument, lunched at a Paris café, hiked the forests of Germany, and rode the waves of Hawaii. Through it all, her love for writing grew. As a retired teacher, Vikki began writing stories to inspire her students and from there, a series of stories was brought to life. After years of creating stories, she is thrilled to share her adventures and love for animals in her first book series, In the Woods. When she is not writing, Vikki spends time with her husband, two grown children, and (of course) her two loving Golden Retrievers on the shores of Virginia. To Vikki Lynn Smith, there is no adventure too big or too small that can't inspire the mind to write!

For more information visit: VikkiLynnSmith.com

I'd like to thank the Williamsburg Writing Group, Dawn, Joanie, and Tori for their encouragement to publish my series, and my family's continued support as I follow my dreams.